ASTERIX AND THE GOLDEN SICKLE

TEXT BY GOSCINNY

DRAWINGS BY UDERZO

TRANSLATED BY ANTHEA BELL AND DEREK HOCKRIDGE

DARGAUD PUBLISHING INTERNATIONAL, LTD.

ASTERIX THE GAUL	0-917201-50-7
ASTERIX AND THE GOLDEN SICKLE	0-917201-64-7
ASTERIX AND THE GOTHS	0-917201-54-X
ASTERIX THE GLADIATOR	0-917201-55-8
ASTERIX AND THE BANQUET	0-917201-71-X
ASTERIX AND CLEOPATRA	0-917201-75-2
ASTERIX AND THE BIG FIGHT	0-917201-58-2
ASTERIX IN BRITAIN	0-917201-74-4
ASTERIX AND THE NORMANS	0-917201-69-8
ASTERIX THE LEGIONARY	0-917201-56-6
ASTERIX AND THE CHIEFTAIN'S SHIELD	0-917201-67-1
ASTERIX AT THE OLYMPIC GAMES	0-917201-61-2
ASTERIX AND THE CAULDRON	0-917201-66-3
ASTERIX IN SPAIN	0-917201-51-5
ASTERIX AND THE ROMAN AGENT	0-917201-59-0
ASTERIX IN SWITZERLAND	0-917201-57-4
ASTERIX AND THE MANSIONS OF THE GODS	0-917201-60-4
ASTERIX AND THE LAUREL WREATH	0-917201-62-0
ASTERIX AND THE SOOTHSAYER	0-917201-63-9
ASTERIX IN CORSICA	0-917201-72-8
ASTERIX AND CAESAR'S GIFT	0-917201-68-X
ASTERIX AND THE GREAT CROSSING	0-917201-65-5
OBELIX & CO.	0-917201-70-1
ASTERIX IN BELGIUM	0-917201-73-6

© DARGAUD EDITEUR PARIS 1962
© HODDER & STOUGHTON LTD. 1975
for the English language text

ISBN 0-917201-64-7

Exclusive licenced distributor for USA:

Distribooks Inc.
8220 N. Christiana Ave.
Skokie, IL 60076-2911
Tel: (708) 676-1596
Fax: (708) 676-1195
Toll-free fax: 800-433-9229

Imprimé en France-Publiphotoffset 93500 Pantin-en mars 1995

Printed in France

GAULISH VILLAGE

COMPENDIUM

LAUDANUM

AQUARIUM

TOTORUM

ARMORICA

BELGICA

LUTETIA

SPQR

GAUL
(ROMAN CONQUEST)
50 B.C.

CELTICA

PROVINCIA

AQUITANIA

The year is 50 BC. Gaul is entirely occupied by the Romans.
Well, not entirely... One small village of indomitable Gauls still
holds out against the invaders. And life is not easy for the
Roman legionaries who garrison the fortified camps of
Totorum, Aquarium, Laudanum and Compendium...

a few of the Gauls ...

Asterix, the hero of these adventures. A shrewd, cunning little warrior; all perilous missions are immediately entrusted to him. Asterix gets his superhuman strength from the magic potion brewed by the druid Getafix...

Obelix, Asterix's inseparable friend. A menhir delivery-man by trade; addicted to wild boar. Obelix is always ready to drop everything and go off on a new adventure with Asterix — so long as there's wild boar to eat, and plenty of fighting.

Getafix, the venerable village druid. Gathers mistletoe and brews magic potions. His speciality is the potion which gives the drinker superhuman strength. But Getafix also has other recipes up his sleeve...

Cacofonix, the bard. Opinion is divided as to his musical gifts. Cacofonix thinks he's a genius. Everyone else thinks he's unspeakable. But so long as he doesn't speak, let alone sing, everybody likes him...

Finally, Vitalstatistix, the chief of the tribe. Majestic, brave and hot-tempered, the old warrior is respected by his men and feared by his enemies. Vitalstatistix himself has only one fear; he is afraid the sky may fall on his head tomorrow. But as he always says, 'Tomorrow never comes.'

Asterix and the Golden Sickle

THE FIERCELY INDEPENDENT LITTLE VILLAGE WHERE ASTERIX AND THE OTHER GAULS LIVE IS AT PEACE...

GOOD HUNTING, ASTERIX?

NOTHING MUCH TODAY...

OBELIX IS HAPPILY AT WORK, CARVING OUT A MENHIR...

THERE'LL ALWAYS BE A GAU-AAU!

CACOFONIX THE BARD IS GIVING THE CHILDREN LESSONS...

WELL, YOUNG MAN, AND INTO HOW MANY PARTS IS GAUL DIVIDED?

$$VIII \times V = XL$$

$$\frac{III}{+\ I} = IV$$

?

IN SHORT, EVERYONE IS CONTENTED. ALL IS PEACE AND PLENTY...

ANOTHER BOAR, OBELIX?

YES, PLEASE!

WHEN SUDDENLY...

OH, BY TOUTATIS!

9

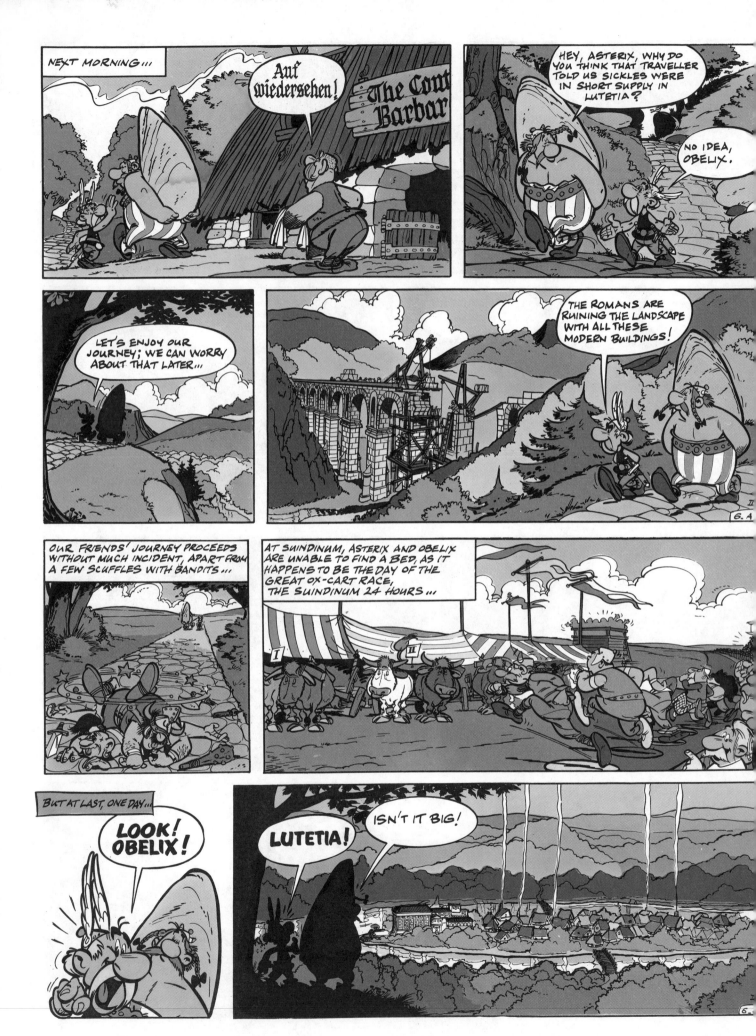

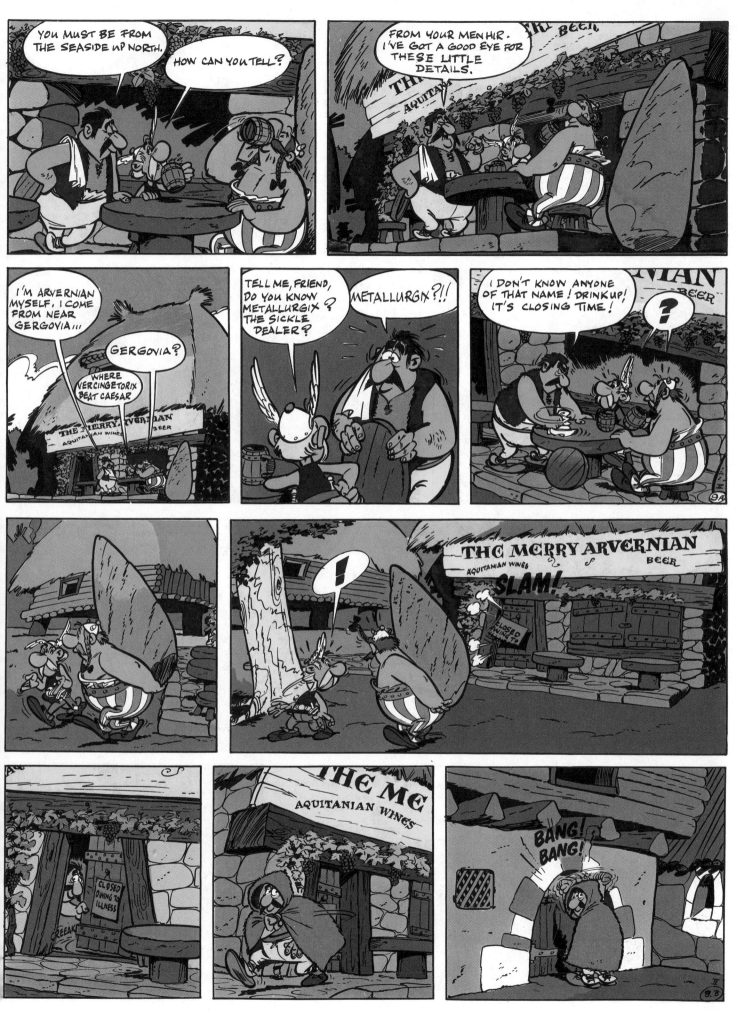

14

17

18

19

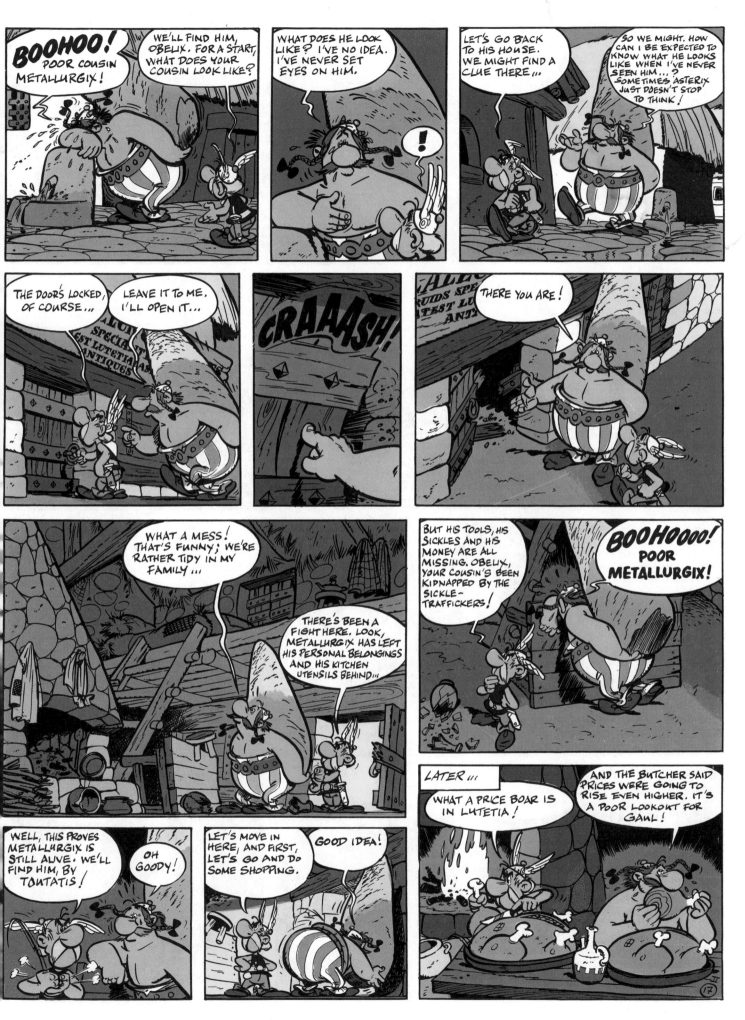

23

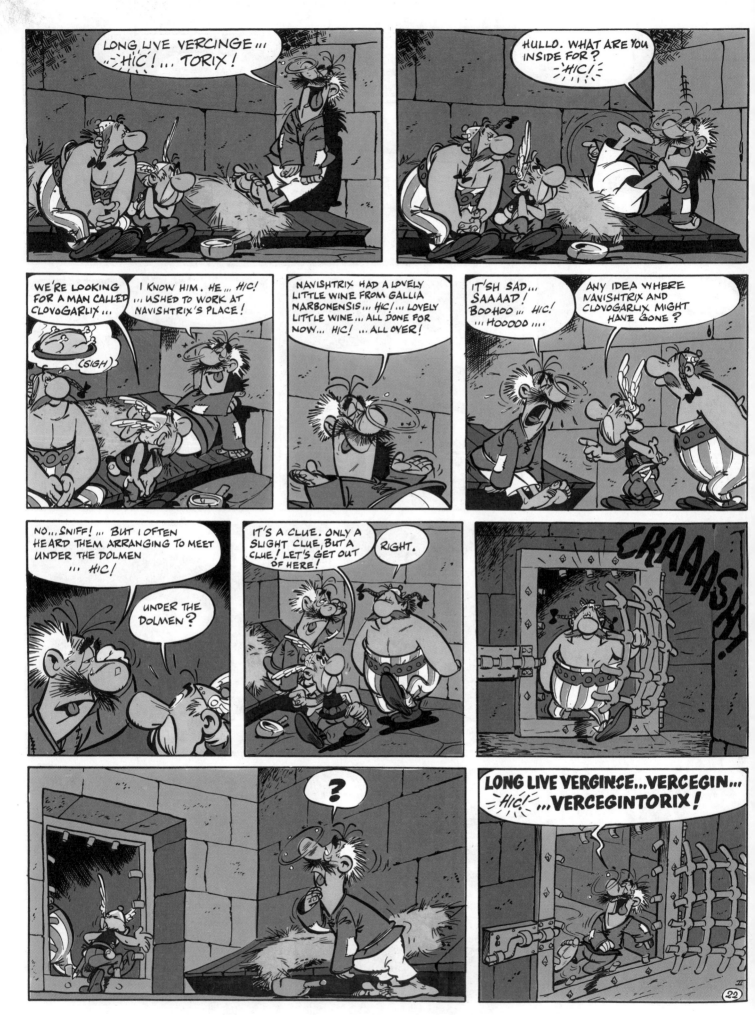

26

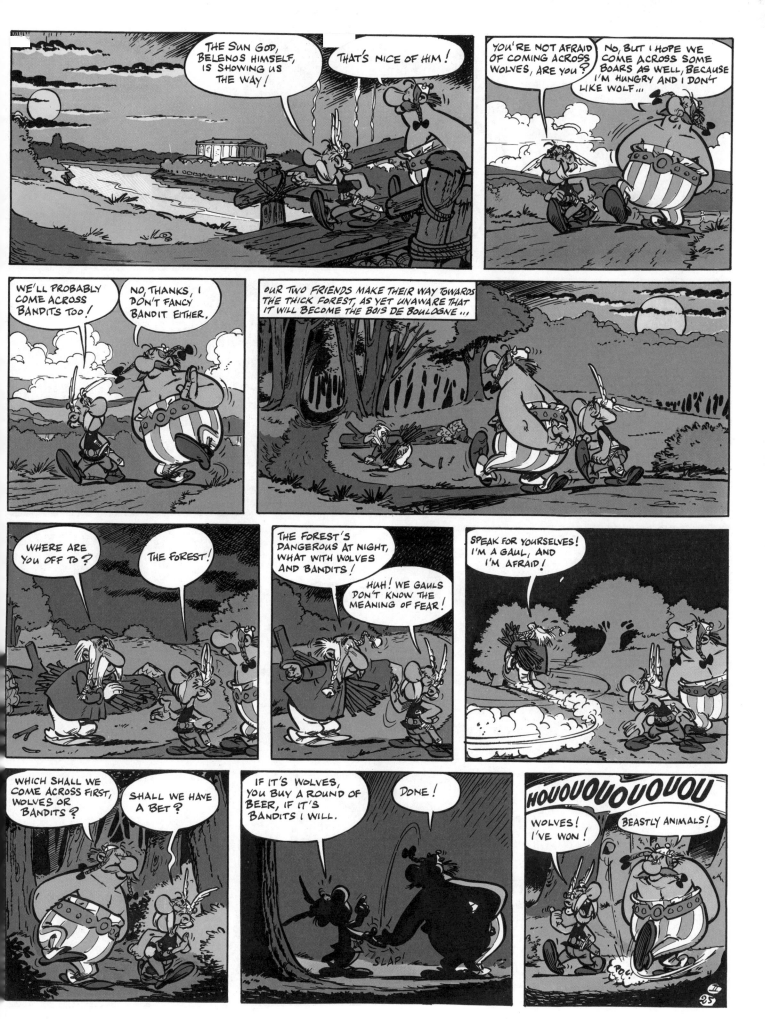

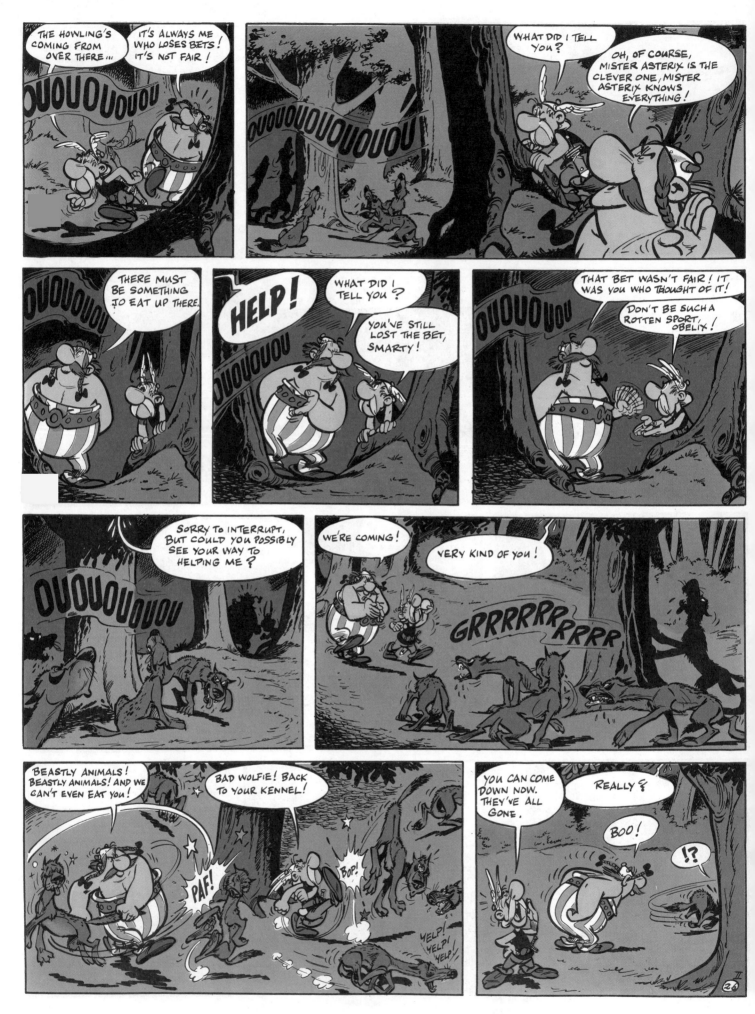

30

31

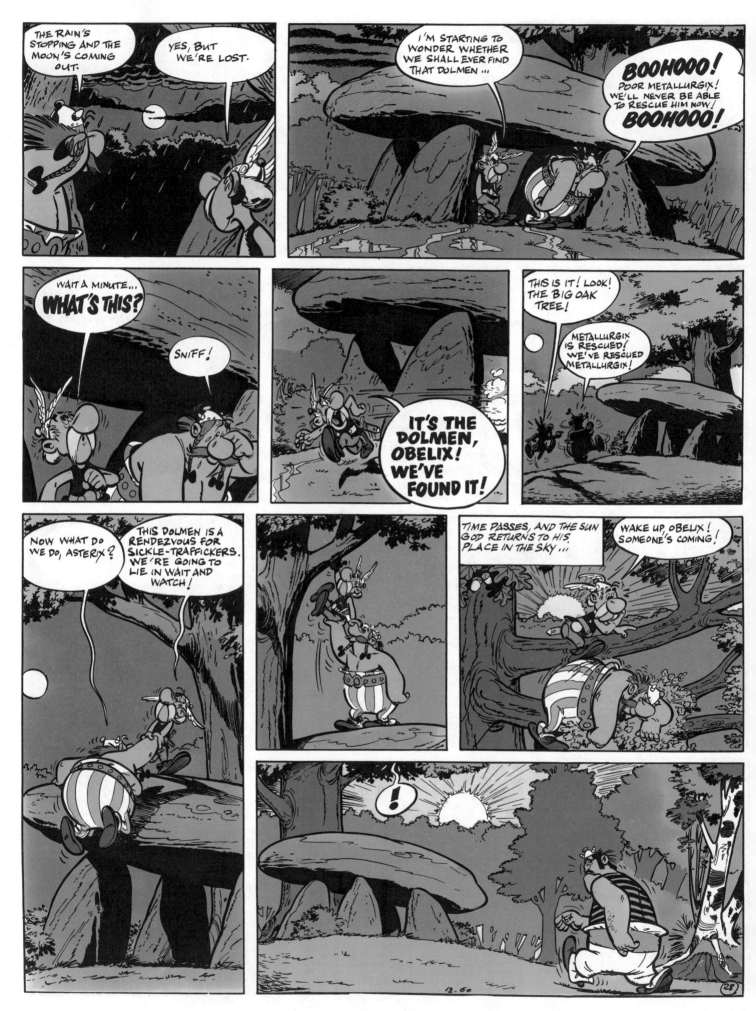

34

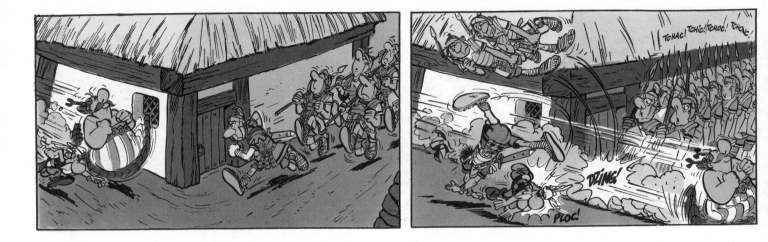

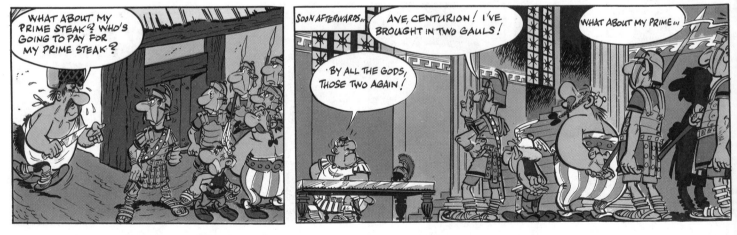

38

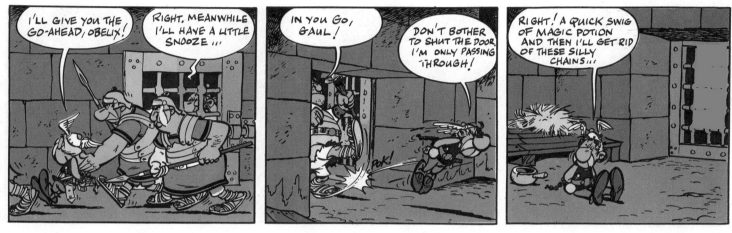

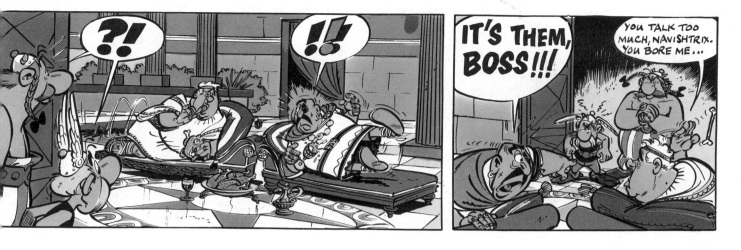